GET WELL SOON, NORRIE!

MEET DUGGEE.

He is a great big cuddly dog. Duggee is in charge of all the fun and adventures at the Clubhouse.

Would you like to meet Duggee's Squirrel Club?

BETTY
is a clever
octopus.

TAG
is a gentle
rhino.

ROLY
is a noisy
little hippo.

HAPPY
is a very happy
crocodile.

NORRIE
Oh! Norrie's not
here today . . .

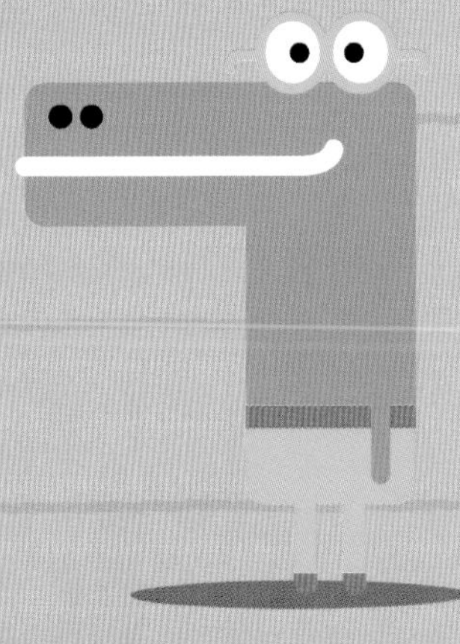

Hello, Squirrels! Oh . . . where's Norrie?

"Woof woof woof," woofs Duggee.

That's right, Duggee. Norrie is a little unwell. She's staying at home in bed. Poor Norrie. What a lot of spots.

The Squirrels want to help Norrie feel better.

"We could do a dance for her," says Tag, doing a dance.

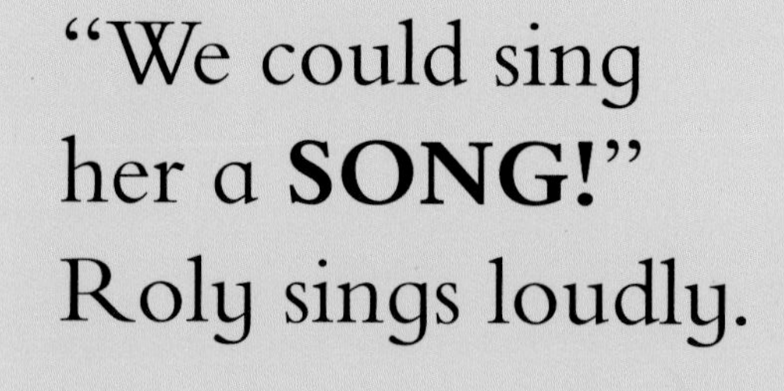

"We could sing her a **SONG!**" Roly sings loudly.

"Or," says Happy, having a **BIG** think, "we could make her a get-well card."

What a good idea, Happy.

"Could you help us, Duggee?" asks Tag.
"Woof," Duggee replies.

Of course Duggee can help.
He has his **GET WELL SOON BADGE**.

"Yay!" cheer the happy Squirrels. They get to work making Norrie's get-well-soon card.

Tag sprinkles glitter . . .

Happy shreds paper . . .

Roly adds feathers . . .

And Betty colours in!

Then they PAINT . . .

. . . and GLUE . . .

. . . and SNIP-SNIP shapes.

Until finally . . .

"WE'VE FINISHED!"

the Squirrels shout.

"Let's take it to Norrie," they say.
"Woof," agrees Duggee.

The Squirrels ride to Norrie's house on Duggee's back.
On the way, they see a rock, a cloud, a bush and . . .

. . . Chew Chew the panda! But she doesn't look well.

"I've got a frightful tummy ache," says Chew Chew. "I'm sooooo hungry."

Poor Chew Chew can't reach all the lovely bamboo. She's only little. "We'll help!" say the Squirrels.

First the Squirrels make a tower to reach as high as they can.

Then Roly breaks off some bamboo for Chew Chew.

"Oh, thank you," says Chew Chew. "My tummy feels better already."

"BYE, CHEW CHEW!" yells Roly.
"Get well soon!" say all the Squirrels.

Who will they see next? Look, it's Frog.

"Hello, Frog," say the Squirrels. Oh dear. Poor Frog doesn't sound well.

"What's wrong, little Frog?" asks Tag.

"He's seasick," says Betty.
"What should we do?" asks Roly.

"Can I help, Duggee?" asks Happy.
"Woof!" Of course you can!

With a great big **SPLASH**,
Happy jumps in and rescues Frog.

Frog feels much better now.
Good work, Happy!

Come on, Squirrels. It's time to be on our way.
"Bye, Frog!" they say. "Get well soon!"

Duggee and the Squirrels are nearly at Norrie's house when . . .

. . . they see Caterpillar.
"Hello, Caterpillar," say the Squirrels.

Oh dear. Caterpillar's got a little cough.

WOW! That was a **BIG** cough.

The Squirrels want to help Caterpillar feel better.

So they make her a lovely bed. "Get well soon," they say.

"Norrie's house!" says Roly.
Hurray! They're here at last.

"Do come in," says Norrie's dad.
"Norrie would love to see you all."

"Hello, Norrie!" the Squirrels say.
"SPOTS!" yells Roly.
He's right. Norrie is still covered in spots.

Betty gives Norrie the card they have made.
"Thank you," says Norrie. "I feel better already."

Look!
Norrie's spots . . .
have disappeared!

Good work, Squirrels! You've helped lots of friends to get well today. You've earned your . . .

"YAY!" cheer the Squirrels. Now there's just time for one more thing before the Squirrels go home . . .

"DUGGEE HUG!"

Do you want to earn your Get Well Soon Badge? Complete these activities, then write your name on the next page and ask an adult to help you to cut it out.

Make a card for someone. It could be a get-well-soon card, or a birthday card, or even just a 'Hello!' card.

Caterpillar makes a BIG cough noise! What's the biggest noise YOU can make?

Can you count all of Norrie's spots? Now cover a piece of paper with lots of dots, too.

Pretend one of your toys is poorly. Make a nice bed for them. Look after them. You could even do a dance, or make up a song for them!

Ribbit like a frog.
And again! Ribbit! Ribbit!

____

earned their

GET WELL SOON BADGE